Dedicated to Pops & Grams

All Things Are Possible

Balboa Press books may be ordered through booksellers or by contacting:

Balboa Press
A Division of Hay House
1663 Liberty Drive
Bloomington, IN 47403
www.balboapress.com
1 (877) 407-4847

ISBN: 978-1-5043-2947-7 (sc)
ISBN: 978-1-5043-2948-4 (e)

Library of Congress Control Number: 2015903941

Print information available on the last page.

Balboa Press rev. date: 04/09/2015

BALBOA.
PRESS
A DIVISION OF HAY HOUSE

Miracle of the Butterscotch Candy

By
Patti Galietta

"It's Thursday after breakfast, Pops," Angel told her grandfather.

Pops didn't even look up. He rattled the pages of his newspaper. "I know the day and time," he answered.

Angel took a baby step closer to Pop's chair, and rested just the tips of her fingers on its arm.

"Aren't we bringing Grams to get her manicure?"

"Of course," Pops mumbled. Angel knew that Pops was not really a gruff man. Grams called it, "his manner, lately" only, to Angel, it didn't seem like Pops used manners lately at all.

Grams came in just then. "And you get your weekly butterscotch candy!" She said, handing a sweater to Angel.

"Gotta have that butterscotch," Pops mumbled.

Angel gave a small, secret smile that showed a missing front tooth. To Angel, a butterscotch candy was a wonderful thing. In fact, for Angel, the whole world was full of wonder, and she wished she knew a way to make Pops feel that, too.

She prayed for it, in fact. Every night, before she closed her eyes, and after she shared the secrets of heart to her mother, who was in Heaven, she prayed that Pops would smile again. He hadn't smiled since Mom's accident.

In the salon parking lot, Pops helped Grams out of the car, and Angel ran ahead to hold the door open for her.

"Afternoon!" Mr. Wong said as Grams swiveled her seat to face her usual manicure table, and Pops made his way to his usual chair beneath the nail polish display.

Mr. Wong waved his hand toward the display, and told Angel, "Pick your color!" It always sounded like an order, and Angel knew it was coming so she was already following where Pops walked.

When she stole a glance at the glass bowl that always held her butterscotch candy, her jaw opened. It was usually bright with red, yellow, and orange wrappers, but today, everything was shades of blues and greens. *Mints!* Angel thought. *There is no butterscotch! Only yucky mints!*

Pops was murmuring, "Pick your color! Pick your color!" Angel looked up at the sour face he was making. He shook his head at her. "There's no color to really 'pick,' is there?"

Pops' bark was harsher than Mr. Wong's. He reached for a reddish shade of orange, so much like the old candy wrappers. It was called "Luscious," and was the only color Grams used.

With a dismissive wave of his hand, Pops gave the little bottle to Angel, to bring to Grams.

Angel's glance probed the candy bowl as she passed it again. If there were even one butterscotch candy in there, its sunburst wrapper would surely stand out, but, no, there was nothing warm and sunny and buttery to see ___ only the cool shades of mints!

Angel skipped back to Pops seated on the sofa, right in front of the coffee table, where the glass bowl sat. Pops was browsing The Readers Magazine, while he fidgeted in his chair waiting for Grams to finish. Angel sat down next to Pops, all the while staring at the *mint* shades in the glass bowl. She thought "BOY!, would I love to see something *Golden* in that bowl. I really believe there has to be *ONE!*" Angel snuggled up to Pops. He put one arm around her while holding tight to the magazine in his other. Feeling safe and at peace, Angel asked, "Gee, Pops, I wish I could find a butterscotch candy in the bowl today. Do you think that can happen?"

"Stop whining!" says Pops. "There isn't any butterscotch candy today. You are talking nonsense! Once Grams is done we will take you to the candy store and you can pick out any candy you like. Now behave and sit still!"

"Pops do you think Mom is watching us now?" Angel asked. She watched the ladies come and go from the nail technician stations. It seemed like an assembly line: first the nail technician station and then on to the dryers, for the final step. Grams was seated next to one of her weekly friends.

Angel always enjoys watching Grams chat with the ladies. Pops barely looked up from the magazine before responding, "I like to think she is watching us, Angel. But, sometimes my belief is not as strong as I would like it to be. I still don't understand why she had to leave us so soon."

"Well, I believe she is right here with us!" Angel exclaimed, "I just know she is!"

Grams was waving from across the room. "I am all finished!" she called softly to Pops. Pops had difficulty hearing and continued to read. "Come on, Pops! It is time for us to go," insisted Angel. "Grams is ready!"

Angel leapt off and ran towards Gram. "Let me see your nails!" she said. "Luscious!"

"*Easy! Easy now! NO Running*!" called Pops as he stood to return his magazine to its rack.

As Pops turned toward the coffee table he noticed a bright sunburst wrapper, all warm and sunny and buttery, sitting on the mound of candy of mints in the glass bowl.

Right on top, as if it were floating in air, sat a *Butterscotch Candy!* Pops picked it up in amazement, and held it in his hand to make sure it was real. "*Yes! It is real!* "he whispered.

With a soft grin, Pops glanced up as if he could see *Heaven* above. He *smiled!*.

Pops then approached Angel and Grams. "Angel," he said, leaning to look into her eyes, "Here is your butterscotch candy."

With excitement Angel grabbed it from his hand. "Where did this come from?" she asked.

With a *twinkle* in his eye, Pops whispered in her ear, "You were right, Angel, Mom *is* here!"

Believe...

CPSIA information can be obtained
at www.ICGtesting.com
Printed in the USA
LVOW01s2027070116

469543LV00020B/178/P

For Angel, the whole world was full of wonder.
She wished she knew a way to make others feel that too.
One routine day and a butterscotch candy is all it took.

The combination of her two passions and her personal experiences helped author Patti Galietta to arrive at writing her story from several perspectives, all of which are enlightening.

Patti is a full-time real estate sales professional specializing in active senior communities. She finds great pleasure in assisting her clients in the transition from one phase of their lives to the next.

Patti has also volunteered as a religious education teacher of grade school children for the past decade. Her relationship with the children and the seniors in addition to her own personal experiences inspired her to write this short story entitled *Miracle of the Butterscotch Candy*.

PATTIGALIETTA.COM

U.S. $10.95

ISBN 978-1-5043-294
51

9 781504 329477

BALBOA
PRESS
A DIVISION OF HAY HOUSE